Bailey
Small, but Fierce

M.L. HAMILTON, AUTHOR

KADYSHA, ILLUSTRATOR

Della June-
I hope you
enjoy Bailey's
adventures. ML
Hamilton
2021

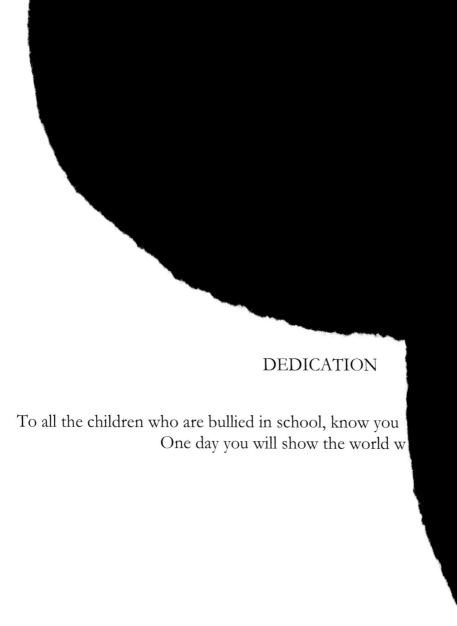

DEDICATION

To all the children who are bullied in school, know you
One day you will show the world w

Bailey was a very small puppy.
She was much smaller than her brothers and sisters.

Bailey's siblings bullied her.
They told her,
"You are too small to be a majestic Golden Retriever. You cannot play with us."

Bailey said,
"I *am* a majestic Golden Retriever. I may be small, but I am fierce.
I will show you who I am."

Her siblings said, "You are a runt. What can you do?"
They pounced on her and knocked her down.
They were so much bigger.

The human lady came and said, "You are too small to be with your siblings.
They pounce on you. They bully you. You are a runt. What can you do?"
She moved Bailey to a new box away from everyone.

Bailey said, "I am not a runt.
I may be small, but I am fierce. I will show you who I am." The lady didn't hear her.
Her siblings didn't hear her. Bailey was alone.

The lady brought people to see her siblings. Bailey barked.
She wanted the people to notice her, but the lady said,
"You do not want that one. She is a runt. What can she do?"

Bailey had to make the people look at her.
She wanted them to know she was a majestic Golden Retriever.
She barked that she was small, but fierce. She tried to tell the people who she was.

The new lady heard Bailey.
She looked at her. She said,
"I want this one. She is small, but fierce. She will be my puppy."

Bailey was so happy. She wiggled.
She gave the new lady kisses. She snuggled into her arms.
Finally, someone saw her for who she was.

The new lady took Bailey to her home.
In the new home, Bailey met her new sibling.
He looked at her and Bailey knew he was a majestic Golden Retriever.

He said, "You are too small to be a majestic Golden Retriever. What can you do?"
Bailey said, "I may be small, but I am fierce. I will show you who I am."

However, Bailey didn't feel well. She didn't feel well at all, so the new lady took Bailey to the veterinarian. The veterinarian looked at Bailey and said, "She is very sick. She is very small. What can she do?"

The lady hugged Bailey tight. She told the veterinarian,
"She may be small, but she is fierce. She will show you who she is."

And Bailey did. She got better. Her new sibling was happy to have a little sister.
He said, "Let's play. You may be small, but you are fierce."
They played a lot of games together.

One of the games her brother liked to play the most was swimming.
Bailey wanted to try swimming,
but she was very small and she couldn't stay above the water.

The lady said, "You are small, but fierce. You will swim, but you need a life vest."
The life vest allowed Bailey to float. Bailey liked her life vest
because then she could play swimming with her brother.

Once Bailey could swim, she decided she would do more.
One day she leaped off the side of the pool.
As she sailed through the air, she thought,
"I may be small, but I am fierce. I will show them who I am."

And Bailey did. She might be small, but she was fierce,
and she was a majestic Golden Retriever.
Bailey could fly.

ABOUT BAILEY

Bailey is a real majestic Golden Retriever. She was the runt of the litter, which means the smallest. When Bailey first came to live with us, she got very sick, but Bailey got better. She is truly small, but fierce. Her vet said, "Bailey may be little, but her personality is big." Bailey's favorite things to do are to annoy her brother, Comet, and play with her best puppy friend, Roxy. However, most of all, Bailey loves to jump into the pool.
I'm pretty sure she thinks she's flying.

VISIT M.L. HAMILTON AT HER WEBSITE

Now that you've finished, visit ML Hamilton at her website: <u>authormlhamilton.net</u> **and sign up for her newsletter. Receive free offers and discounts once you sign up!**

The Complete *Peyton Brooks' Mysteries* Collection:
Murder in the Painted Lady, Volume 0
Murder on Potrero Hill Volume 1
Murder in the Tenderloin Volume 2
Murder on Russian Hill Volume 3
Murder on Alcatraz Volume 4
Murder in Chinatown Volume 5
Murder in the Presidio Volume 6
Murder on Treasure Island Volume 7

Peyton Brooks FBI Collection:
Zombies in the Delta Volume 1
Mermaids in the Pacific Volume 2
Werewolves in London Volume 3
Vampires in Hollywood Volume 4
Mayan Gods in the Yucatan Volume 5
Haunts in Bodie Volume 6
Menehune in Kauai Volume 7

Zion Sawyer Cozy Mystery Collection:
Cappuccino Volume 1
Café Au Lait Volume 2
Espresso Volume 3
Caffe Macchiato Volume 4
Americano Volume 5

The Avery Nolan Adventure Collection:
Swift as a Shadow Volume 1
Short as Any Dream Volume 2
Brief as Lightning Volume 3
Momentary as a Sound Volume 4

The Complete *World of Samar* Collection:
The Talisman of Eldon Emerald Volume 1
The Heirs of Eldon Volume 2
The Star of Eldon Volume 3
The Spirit of Eldon Volume 4
The Sanctuary of Eldon Volume 5
The Scions of Eldon Volume 6
The Watchers of Eldon Volume 7
The Followers of Eldon Volume 8
The Apostles of Eldon Volume 9
The Renegade of Eldon Volume 10
The Fugitive of Eldon, Volume 11

Stand Alone Novels:
Ravensong
Jaguar
Serenity

The Year of Discovery
January
February
March
April
May
June
July
August
September
October
November
December

The Moon Light Trilogy
The Moon Thief

COMING IN 2021

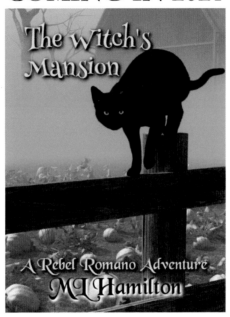

MID-GRADE READER

Rebel Romano always avoided the haunted house on the corner, but when some older kids from school chase her home, she has no choice but to take refuge in the yard of the scary mansion.

Crossing the boundary onto the witch's property begins a series of adventures that will teach Rebel that gossip isn't always true, and sometimes the things we think we fear are not scary at all.

Made in the USA
San Bernardino, CA
04 January 2020

62651594R00015